Verses

By

Susan M. Garlock

God is always with us no matter what

The following story is fiction. Names, characters, places and incidents are all products of the author's imagination.

Verses are from the Bible, the word of God

Cover photo by "Scott Garlock Photography" Macon, NC

Cover photo title: "A Magnolia Morning"

www. Scottgarlockphotography.com

All rights reserved and copyrighted in 2015

From an 1849 Bible

The words of the Lord are pure words: as silver tried in a furnace of earth, purified seven times.

Psalm 12:6

Verses

Chapter 1

Only two days left of her fiscal year ending in the month of June, and Julie still had a lot to do at her bookstore. She needed to sell a couple dozen more books and she would be in the black for her second year in business. Hopefully putting up the "Book Sale" sign in her store window would bring the promise of more sales. Julie had put all of her savings into her bookstore, and there were times, when she wondered if she would ever be able to pay the monthly rent. Still she was proud of the fact that she was only in her late twenties and she had accomplished her dream of having her very own bookstore.

When Julie was attending business school, one of her classmates who lived in North Carolina had invited her to come for a visit. Soon after graduation Julie visited her friend and she fell in love with the beautiful state and its quaint little towns. It was on that memorable visit that Julie happened to be in the small town of Warrenton, North Carolina, when she saw a sign in a downtown store window that said, "For Rent." She immediately contacted the store's owner, signed a lease, and it was only afterwards that she thought to herself, can I really do this.

One of the keys to Julie's bookstore success, was not having to buy so many books directly from the publishers. She had decided to instead go another route and have people bring their unwanted and old and used books to her. Most of the time her customers just wanted to get rid of their books and they dropped them off at Julie's book drop. The book drop was located on the side of her store and people could just drive up and place their books in the slot and go their merry way. For Julie it was always exciting to see the different kinds of books that people didn't want anymore. There were the usual romance and mystery paperbacks, a little worn, but would always fetch a few dollars. Sometimes she would be lucky enough to find in her book drop some new titles that were right off the press and didn't have much wear. Julie would promptly place those books in her front window to draw in customers. Occasionally there were some books that were not suitable for the store and she would quickly put those in the trash. The books that Julie liked to receive the most were the vintage and antique books that people would find in their basements, garages and attics. If the books weren't literally falling apart, she would check to see if all the pages were intact, and then she would put a protective sleeve over the book and place it in her antique and rare book section in her store. Sometimes the books would come from estate sales or yard sales, and they were always the books that didn't sell, so people would bring them to Julie's book drop. Julie looked the books over thoroughly and some she would keep but some would end up in the pile that she would donate to the Goodwill Store.

   Today Julie's book drop was completely full and she was thrilled with more inventory for her store. But with all the other things she needed to do the books would just have to wait to be cataloged and inventoried later. She loaded the books into some boxes she kept near the book drop, and as she was putting them in, she came across a couple of very old books that had a little bit of a musty smell. One of the books was a huge Bible. Instantly she felt sad that someone would actually throw away an old Bible. She had no way of knowing who the people were that dropped off the books at her store. She also didn't have a security camera that would show who they were. But then she thought that maybe the person that dropped off the old Bible knew she would take care of it and she knew she would.

Even though Julie had more important things to do, she sat down with the Bible on her blue and red braided throw rug on the stores hardwood floor. She carefully ran her fingers over the heavy old leathery bound Bible which looked to measure at least twelve inches in size. She could tell that the Bible had originally two metal clasps to hold it together but one of the clasps was missing. The one that was left was doing its best to hold the extra-large Bible together. She also noticed that the Bible had a string of twine tied securely around its middle. Probably to help the only clasp that was doing double duty keeping the old Bible in one piece. People in the past that were fortunate enough to own their own Bible were very protective of it. If pages would happen to come loose from the binding, they would simply fold the pages in half and tuck them in someplace in the Bible. They were faithfully trying to keep their family Bible complete.

When Julie untied the twine that held the Bible, it immediately released a puff of dry dust in her face and she reacted with a sneeze. With the twine gone, she carefully undid the old metal clasp and opened up the Bible. She removed and laid aside all the loose pages that were tucked in the front of the Bible. Thankfully one of them was the intact title page with no tears. As a book dealer, the most important part of a book is the title page. She laid it aside and looked at the page numbers on each of the loose pages, and they were all there, including the end of the book pages that had also come loose from the binding.

Julie picked up the title page again and she saw that the date of publication of the Bible was 1849, long before the Civil War. She looked in the back of the Bible to see if there were any births, deaths or other notes on the back inside cover. Most people would usually record their family events by posting them in their Bibles, but this one however, did not have a single name on the inside covers. There were however several Bible verses handwritten on the back cover. It left Julie wondering who the owner of the Bible was or where it had come from.

Before she could look for more clues in the Bible, time had gotten away from her and someone knocked on the store's front door. Julie quickly picked up the big Bible and put it on a nearby shelf.

Then she went to open the door and it was one of her favorite customers, Mrs. Clayborn, who was always looking for a few steamy romance novels to buy.

Verses

Chapter 2

After Mrs. Clayborn left with a bag full of paperback novels, Julie had all but forgotten the Bible on the storeroom shelf. Two more customers came into the store, one that bought a copy of John Grisham's newest novel that Julie found in her book drop last week, and a customer looking for several older looking books to put in their living room. They wanted to decorate their house all in antiques. Julie didn't mind that the books were being used as props and not intended to be read. She was pleased that her books would be on display and that they would be well taken care of.

It was after twelve o'clock, and well past the usual time that Julie would stop to eat her lunch, when a man with dark brown hair came into her store and began browsing in the old book section. He was wearing a dress shirt with jeans that seem to fit very well and he wasn't wearing a wedding ring. But more important, he was very handsome.

"May I help you look for something?" Julie anxiously asked.

"I'm fine, just going to check out the old books." The gentleman said.

"Ok but let me know if I can be of any help." Julie said as she proceeded to unwrap her peanut butter and strawberry jelly sandwich. It was the same thing she ate every day because it didn't need refrigeration, and right now, she didn't have the money to buy a refrigerator for the store. She would always partner up her sandwich with either an apple or an orange. Sometimes it made her feel like when she was back in grade school, and back in those days you didn't have Oscar Myer Lunchables, and a peanut butter sandwich was the only thing your mother would put in your lunch.

Julie got one bite out of her sandwich when the interesting customer asked, "Do you have any old religious books?"

"I do, as a matter of fact I have several old hymnals and prayer books on the upper shelf to your left. I do not sell Bibles, I don't feel comfortable doing that. If I come across a Bible I try to find its original owner, and if I can't, I donate them."

"That's very admirable of you, and I respect your decision."

"It's just what I do." Julie responded with a blush and pushed her half eaten sandwich under her counter and hopefully out of site.

"I'm sorry, I should have introduced myself. I'm the new pastor at the Church of Christ on Second Street. My name's Matthew Lewiston."

"Pleased to meet you Mr. Lewiston, my name's Julie Devers and welcome to my bookstore."

"Nice to meet you too but please call me Matt."

Julie watched as the man continued to browse the old books and then pulled several old hymnals and placed them on her counter.

"I think these will do for now, I love collecting the old hymnals, along with Bibles and other religious material, it's kind of a hobby of mine."

"I will definitely keep that in mind Pastor, and if you want, I can notify you when I get more of those types of books in. Just leave your email address on my mailing list and I will be more than happy to let you know." Julie said as she couldn't keep her eyes off the tall and strikingly handsome man standing in front of her counter.

"I will do that, now if you can give me a total on what I owe you, I will be on my way."

"Oh, I'm sorry, oh what the heck, the books are yours, call it a welcome to our town of Warrenton gift."

"You don't have to do that."

"I know I don't but I just did."

"Gee thanks for your kindness, I will take very good care of your books."

"I'm sure you will, and you have a good day Mr. Lewiston, I mean Matt."

"You too Julie."

After Matt left the bookstore, Julie couldn't help but stare out the front window hoping to get another look at the new pastor in town. Her insides were fluttering around like butterflies. Her cell phone rang and she looked at the caller ID and it was her mother calling and it brought her back to reality.

"Hello mother, what's up?"

"Just calling to see how you're doing dear, it's raining here today, and I don't feel much like going anywhere so I'm catching up on my calls."

"Its ok mom, everyone needs a day to sit back and relax. Why don't you read some of the books that I sent you in the mail?" Julie said knowing full well that her mother wasn't much into reading books.

"I might do that, but what are you up to today, is the store keeping you busy? Wish I was there to keep you company. Is anything happening in that little town of yours?"

"I am very busy mom, I have a lot to do before the end of my fiscal year, and no, not much happening here." Julie responded and didn't want to discuss the new pastor in her town. If she did, her mother would be hounding her constantly, and wanting to know all about him. Even though she missed her mother, Julie was kind of glad that her mother lived up in Philadelphia. "Why don't you call some of your friend's mother, maybe you could all get together for lunch today?"

"I'll think about it, I was just checking up on you dear."

"I know mom, but I really have to go, I have so much to do today. But I will definitely call you back as soon as I have some free time."

"Please do that. You know your right dear, I think I will call and see if Janice wants to have lunch today. You take care of yourself, love you."

"Love you too mom."

Julie made herself busy cataloging more books, but at the same time, she was starting to feel a little guilty about her mom. After her father passed away and she moved to Warrenton, North Carolina, it had to have been hard on her mother being alone. It was during Julie's last year of school that her father had a fatal heart attack. She missed him terribly. He was the one person she could go to with just about anything that was on her mind. Her mother was always just a little too busy with her friends, her clubs and trying to keep up with the neighbors. Julie knew that the best thing for her to do was to get out from underneath her mother's roof and start her own life. She took the money that was left to her from her father's will and used that money to start her very own business.

Several more customers came into the store and Julie sold more of her books and at that point she knew she had made her quota for the year. It was after closing time when she was tidying up the backroom of her bookstore when she remembered the old Bible sitting on the shelf. She could have kicked herself for not mentioning and showing the Bible to the new pastor. Even though she didn't have a chance to find out who the Bible had belonged to, the pastor might have been able to help shed some light on it. She sat the Bible on a folding table that she had bought at the Goodwill store when she was setting up her business and she opened it up. She carefully leafed through the thousands of pages to see if someone had left something identifiable inside. In the past Julie had found multiple items in other old books. She would find recipes from magazines used as bookmarkers along with family newspaper clippings. One time she found a vintage baseball card that was in mint condition that had been used as a bookmarker in an old medical book. When she did the research on the baseball player she found that the player had played back in the 1940's. Unfortunately he was not so famous and the card was only worth about thirty dollars. Julie decided to keep the card until someday it would be worth a lot more.

    As Julie looked through the Bible she was amazed at the steel engravings. Pictures in the old Bibles, especially the much larger ones, were made from a process called steel engraving. These pictures were always in black and white and the detail and clarity in them was beautiful. Some people, to Julie's dismay, would dismantle an old vintage Bible just to sell the pictures on internet sites like eBay. This practice always made Julie furious and sad that someone would actually destroy a beautiful Bible just to make a profit. Thankfully no one had taken out any of the pictures in this Bible. As she turned the pages, Julie found an old bookmarker that had been crocheted with tiny faded pink and white threads. She left the bookmarker in the Bible where she had found it but she made a note on her handy tablet about the bookmarker. Julie concluded that the Bible was indeed intact with all of its steel engravings, end papers, title and date page, and especially the leather bound front and back covers. The Bible would bring a lot of money but Julie would never sell it. So, until she could find more clues as to the owner of the Bible, and return it to its rightful owner, she would just have to keep it safe on her backroom shelf.

Verses

Chapter 3

Julie woke up thinking about the new pastor in town. She had noticed that when he was in her store that he was not wearing a wedding ring, but of course that doesn't mean that he might not be engaged, or for that matter, have a girlfriend. Most men of the cloth, except for priests, are usually married. But Julie was hoping that Matt had just not found the right person yet. She was thinking about her own love life which wasn't all that impressive. Her mother once fixed her up with the son of one of her friends. That lasted about three dates because she just couldn't stand him any longer. All his conversations were about himself, probably to try to impress her, but it didn't work. If she heard one more story, about how he was his company's number one salesman, she was going to throw up.

On the way to the bookstore, Julie took a detour and went down Second Street to scout out the Church of Christ. When she was a little girl her mother had taken her to a Methodist Church in Philadelphia. But it only lasted until someone in the church asked her mother if she would host a ladies group for lunch, and her mother didn't think that their house would be good enough for entertaining, so they never went back. Since that time her father had moved up the ladder at work and they had moved twice. Finally, much to her mother's delight, settling into a much larger home. Her mother now owns four sets of silverware and four sets of good china with matching crystal for just about every occasion. Today she host all kinds of parties and events.

Julie slowly turned into the parking lot of the church so that she could get a better view of the beautiful white church with its big wood doors on the front. She sat quietly in her car just looking at the church. She thought it looked like a very nice church with its perfect steeple sitting on top and big stained glass windows. To herself she was thinking that maybe someday she would visit the church and hear to one of Matt's sermons. It wouldn't hurt her and maybe it just might do her some good.

Arriving at the bookstore Julie unlocked the front door and put her open sign in the window. She then quickly went to make some fresh hot coffee for her customers. She was way ahead on her sales now so any sales today would be a bonus. No one was in the store, so just for fun, she brought out the old Bible from the storeroom and placed it gently on the counter to study it a little more. After a while there was more than one curious shopper who was interested in the antique Bible. One customer even offered a considerable amount of money for it, but Julie had to say no. She explained that she was going to keep it. Even though that was not the truth, and she didn't like lying, she would never sell a Bible.

Julie was busy looking at the pictures of biblical events that played out in black and white inside the Bible when someone tapped her on the shoulder. It startled her to the point where she jumped back in her chair.

"You must have been a million miles away." Matt said as he smiled at Julie.

"More like thousands of years." Julie replied and smiled back at Matt and thought how wonderful it would be to run her fingers through that wavy brown hair.

"That's quite a Bible you have there, looks like it weighs more than you."

"It is quite heavy and it's very cumbersome to carry from room to room."

"Mind if I look at it with you?"

"Not at all, maybe you can help me with something."

"At your service, what can I do for you?"

"Well, like I told you yesterday, I do not sell Bibles. I always like to try to find the Bible's owner if that's possible. But this 1849 Bible is a mystery. It doesn't have any names in the back like most family Bibles do. It's sad but I have no idea who the family was that owned this beautiful Bible. The only clues I have so far is an old crocheted bookmarker and a list of biblical verses handwritten on the inside of the back cover." Julie answered with that butterfly thing in her stomach coming back.

"Let's take a look at those Bible verses and see what they say, they might be able to give us some kind of clue."

Julie liked the fact that Matt used the word us it made her feel a little warm inside. Matt carefully turned to the back cover of the Bible and found the list of fifteen verses. He copied them down on a small notepad which he conveniently carried in his pocket.

"They're interesting verses but I really need to study them a little more. I'm sorry but I'm going to have to leave here soon, but I'll tell you what, I promise I'll get back to you on these verses. Maybe I'll find something out by studying each of the verses separately. Favorite verses can tell a lot about a person. How about if we meet for lunch tomorrow and we try to figure out this little mystery?"

"Oh I'm sorry Matt, but I can't leave the store, I don't have anyone to watch it when I'm not here. However, if you want, we can have lunch right here at the bookstore and I'll pack an extra peanut butter & jelly sandwich. Sorry that's all I can offer, I don't have a refrigerator in the store."

"I can do one better, I'll bring lunch to you, what do you like, Chinese, Mexican, Italian or good ole American fare?"

"Whatever you like Matt, I'm not that particular. Anything would be better than peanut butter and jelly."

"Then it's a date say around one o'clock?"

"That would be wonderful and I'm really looking forward to it."

Julie distinctly heard Matt whistling something as he left the bookstore. The butterflies were still fluttering around in her stomach, as she peeked over the stacks of books in her store window, to watch Matt get in his car and disappear down Main Street. As soon as he was out of sight Julie got busy sprucing up the store and straightening up all the misplaced books. She wanted her store to look its best for when the pastor returned the next day.

Verses

Chapter 4

Tomorrow couldn't come fast enough for Julie. She set her clock for an earlier time than usual and then she spent that time picking out something nice to wear to her bookstore. Her wardrobe was a bit thin, she didn't want to pack a lot of clothes when she left her mother's house a couple of years ago, so only the practical and bare necessities were in her apartment closet. She picked out blue slacks and a blue and white stripped summer blouse. She fixed her long blonde hair up with clips, put on some fresh make-up, and she was out the door long before her usual departure time. She remembered at the last minute that she needed to get gas. So she allowed enough time for that and for a cup of freshly made coffee from the convenient store down the road. She could have waited until she got to work and made coffee for herself, and for her customers, but she thought she would treat herself on this special day.

Julie tried to make the morning go fast, as she watched the clock until it was a quarter till one, and then she started watching the front door of her store. It wasn't until one fifteen that the pastor came hurrying in the door carrying two large bags of takeout food.

"Sorry I'm late, had to stand in line at two different places." Matt said as he put the two bags on Julie's counter.

"You went to two places?"

"Yep, wasn't sure about the first one so decided to swing by another."

"You didn't have to do that Matt. I would have liked whatever you brought."

"Not sure about that my taste buds can easily give anyone a good case of heartburn."

"Well, regardless, I'm so starved I think I could eat the bag that's holding all that food."

Matt and Julie enjoyed eating the delicious Italian ravioli, and along with the Italian food, Matt even ate one of the cheeseburgers that he thought to buy at the last moment. He said that she could take whatever was left home with her because he needed to stop at the hospital on his way home to visit a few patients from his church.

It was well past three o'clock when they finally were able to clear the counter and make room for the old Bible. While Julie waited on a customer that wanted a couple of mystery detective books, Matt studied the many steel engravings that depicted stories he knew all too well. He had planned many of his sermons on those exact stories of the Bible. When Julie was finished with her customer Matt told her that his research of the Bible verses at his house didn't pan out. He said that he looked at all fifteen verses and he didn't come up with any possible clues.

"So you're saying that none of the verses were similar in nature?"

"Just the fact that the first verse starts with Genesis and the last one Revelation. All the other verses are in between. I studied each verse separately, but nothing unusual, they just seemed to be randomly picked out. None of them were the popular verses that we all know and love. Also you have to realize that the Bibles of today have a different language than a Bible from the year 1849. It will be interesting to see how the verses read in this old Bible.

"Show me Matt, I have to admit, I don't even know any verses in the Bible. Wish I did, but unfortunately, I didn't grow up hearing the Bible like most people. I only attended church when I was a little girl and that wasn't for very long."

"I would be glad to show you the verses maybe you might see something that I might have missed."

"I'm not sure about that."

Matt took out his notepad with the list of fifteen verses on it and then he opened the 1849 Bible to the first verse. It was Genesis 1:1. He noticed right away that the chapters were in Roman numerals.

"Wow, didn't count on that, makes it a little harder to look up the chapters unless you know Roman numerals. But don't worry I can easily look up the Roman numerals that we're not sure of on your computer. That is, if you don't mind, and then we can convert them to numbered chapters."

"Go for it." Julie replied.

After converting the Roman numeral chapters to numbers for all the verses, Matt continued, and right away he saw that the "O" in "God" in Genesis

1:1 was circled. He wrote down the "O" on his notepad next to the verse. The next verse was Leviticus 19:10. In that verse Matt noticed that the "U" in the word "thou" was circled so he wrote that on his notepad. He turned to the next verse that was Samuel 3:8 and there was an "R" circled in the word "arose." Now Julie was getting into it and she watched as Matt turned to the next verse that was Chronicles 35:15 and there was a "D" in the name "David" circled. Matt continued. The next verse was Ezra 9:14 and the "R" in the word "break" was circled. Next was Psalm 75:2 and the "Y" in the word "uprightly" was circled. The next verse was in the book of Proverbs and the verse was 15:12 and the "C' in the word "scorner" was circled. Next was Isaiah 29:7 and the "R" in the word "Ariel" was circled. By now both Matt and Julie were getting excited to find the next letter. The next book was Jeremiah 42:6 and the "E" in the word "obey" was circled. Next was the verse Ezekiel 4:9 and the letter "E" in "thee" was found. The next verse was from the New Testament and the book of Matthew. The verse was 17:25 and the "K" in "thinkest" was circled. Julie laughed at the word "thinkest."

"See I told you some of the words would be a little strange and funny sounding from an 1849 Bible." Matt said as turned to the next verse and it was Mark 6:3 and the "R" was circled in "carpenter." In the book of Luke, verse 16:13, the letter "O" in "love" was circled. The next to last book was John 18:1 and the "A" in the word "garden" was circled. The last book in the list of fifteen verses was the last book in the New Testament and the Bible. The book was Revelation and the verse was 12:4 and the "D" in the word "dragon" was circled.

"Wait Matt, there are three more verses written at the very bottom of the cover but you can barely see them. It looks like Proverbs 16:9, Psalm 32:7 and Galatians 3:23. Let's look up those verses too." Julie suggested as she saw the excitement in Matt's eyes. Before they could look up three more verses a customer came into the store.

"I'll have to take care of my customer but I'll be right back." Julie whispered to Matt. "I wouldn't miss this for the world."

By the time Matt flipped the heavy pages to look up the book of Proverbs in the Old Testament,

Julie was back beside him. She was amazed how quickly he knew exactly where to go in the Bible, but of course he would, being a Minister of God and the Bible. The first verse of the newly found three verses was Proverbs 16:9 and the verse said, "A man's heart deviseth his way: but the Lord directeth his steps." The word "steps" in the verse was circled.

"Wow, that's interesting, there is actually a word circled instead of just letters." Julie said as she looked at Matt as he wrote down the circled word "steps" on his notepad.

The next verse was Psalm 32:7 and the verse in the 1849 Bible read, "Thou art my hiding- place; thou shalt preserve me from trouble; thou shalt compass me about with songs of deliverance. Selah." And the words, "Thou art my hiding-place" were circled in the verse. The last verse was Galatians 3:23 and it read, "But before faith came, we were kept under the law, shut up unto the faith which should afterwards be revealed." The words, "shut up" and "be revealed" were circled. There were no other verses handwritten on the inside back cover of the Bible and there were no clues yet to whoever the Bible belonged to.

"Ok Sherlock Holms, what have you written down on your notepad?" Julie was anxious to know.

"Well, the letters that were circled in the list of fifteen books of the Bible are, ourdrycreekroad. I'm pretty sure that's an address."

"I think you're right Matt, what were the words circled in the last three verses again?"

"The first circled word was, "steps," then the words, "Thou art my hiding- place" and in the last verse the words circled were, "shut up" and "be revealed."

"Gee that all sounds a little creepy, what do you think?" Julie asked but was interrupted with the sound of the bell ringing on her shop's door and another customer coming into the store. Julie happily helped the customer who was looking for a few gardening books and then another customer came in and was looking for a book on crockpot cooking. Julie was busy with her two customers for the next half hour but from time to time she would look over her shoulder and see Matt studying his notes. He was flipping through the old Bible checking rechecking to make sure he wrote down the right words.

When her customers left the bookstore, Julie hurried over to Matt and back to the large Bible sitting on her counter.

"Did you find any more words Matt?"

"No, just those strange words from the verses in the back. When do you close today? It would be a beautiful day for a ride in the country, can you close early and take a ride with me so we can find this address? Of course, it might not even be an address from around here, it could be from some other state for all we know."

"I would love to close early, after all, it's less than two hours before I usually close my store. I have a navigation system in my car with GPS capability so we can use that to find the address, that is, if it exits." Julie anxiously responded and getting excited about going on a drive with Pastor Matt.

Julie looked out the door to see if anyone was coming towards her store. Then she quickly put her closed sign in the window and she and the Pastor left the store before any more customers could come in. They hopped in Julie's car and Matt entered the address in her navigation system and they left to explore wherever Dry Creek Road would lead them.

Verses

Chapter 5

As they were traveling down the road, Julie asked Matt why he wanted to be a pastor, especially in a small town like Warrenton. He explained that he really had no choice in the matter, that when the ministry presented him with a calling, no matter where that calling would take you, it was where God wanted you to be. Julie was impressed with Matt's dedication as a pastor. Matt asked Julie why she had set up a bookstore in Warrenton, and she explained how it had always been her dream to have her very own bookstore. Julie loved books and she told Matt that when her father died, and left her money, she used it to start her own bookstore business.

With Julie's navigation system it didn't take long to find a road that was called Dry Creek Road. It was located about ten miles outside of town. The road was not well traveled, and unfortunately for Julie's clean car, it was also a dirt road. There hadn't been any rain for days so the car kicked up quite a dust storm behind them as they drove down the seemingly deserted road.

"This road looks like it's going to be coming to a dead end soon, are you sure you want to continue Julie?"

"Of course I do, I haven't had this much fun in a long time." Julie responded as she watched the woods for any signs of houses along the road.

"I don't see any mail boxes, and if there were a house on this road from that time period, you wouldn't find house numbers because there weren't any back then." Matt suggested.

"So, the only thing we can go on is that at one time there might have been a house located on this old dirt road. Stop!" Julie quickly said as she strained to see something in the dense woods.

"What is it? Did you see something?"

"I think so, back up a little. I think I saw a big house but with all the trees and the overgrown brush, it's really hard to see."

"Let's get out and explore just a little, there's no trespassing sign, and for what I can see there are no fences or gates to stop us from just going on a little hike." Matt said as he parked the car on the side of the dirt road.

"I'm game, I have walking shoes on so I can do a little hiking."

Matt locked the car and he and Julie went exploring on a property that they didn't know what to expect or who even owned it. They searched for an opening, but no matter where they looked, it was thick briar patches and overgrown bushes everywhere. It was so dense that Matt had to use the back of his arm to push away the brush and overgrown weeds that had covered the once used dirt path. His fresh new shirt he had put on that morning to impress Julie, was now getting snagged on thorns and briar bushes. His arm was now covered with tiny scratches and some of them were even bleeding. Just when he was going to suggest that they turn around and go back, the dirt path opened up to a shockingly run down old plantation house. Even with the sun shining on the house it didn't do it any justice. It was extremely weathered and gray looking and the weeds had grown so tall around the house that you could hardly see the front steps on the porch. Looking at the front of the house you could just barely see pieces of curtains still hanging on the inside of the windows. A couple of the windows had broken windowpanes and they were unfortunately exposing the house to the elements. Julie stood in awe of the estate and her mind ran wild thinking about the family that had once lived there. She wondered also if there had been children living in the house. She looked at the overgrown fields for as far as she could see and she wondered if they grew tobacco or cotton in the fields. It looked as though, and not that many years ago, that someone had planted the fields. Of course it didn't mean that people were living in the house. It could have been a relative or just someone who leased the fields for planting from whoever owned the estate.

"Well, now we know, this house looks to be the only house that is on Dry Creek Road, and whoever lived in this house might have had something to do with the old Bible." Matt concluded as he studied the grounds and saw what was left of three small log houses adjacent to the house and they were in bad condition. He figured they must have been slave quarters for the family that lived in the bigger house.

"I'm going to take some pictures with my cell phone before we leave." Julie announced as she clicked several pictures from different angles of the house and several pictures of the out buildings. She just couldn't believe that the house at one time was someone's beautiful home. Now it was just a deserted structure left to the elements to simply rot away.

"What do say we leave this big ole house and head back to town? I probably should do some visiting with a couple of our parishioners that are at the hospital before I go home."

"Yea, as much as I would like to stay and explore a little more, it's probably wise that we do more research on the house and maybe even try to locate the owner for permission to be on his property." Julie replied.

"That could be a whole other problem. Some of these old North Carolina homes and land have been left in wills to second, third and even fourth cousins. Many don't even know they own property, and those that do, don't want others to know about it. Probably because of the taxes they would owe on the property. That's just the way people are around here. So, on that thought, you might never learn anything more about this old house."

"That's so sad, such a waist. I'm sure there has to be someone who knows something about this property." Julie said as she and Matt retraced their steps and returned to her car.

"Good luck with that." Matt replied as they turned the car around on the dirt road and drove back to town.

Matt and Julie switched cars back at the bookstore. They both said that they had a good time on their adventure and Julie told Matt how much she enjoyed her lunch. She told Matt he could stop in anytime at the bookstore to talk about the Bible verses. Matt accepted her invitation and then he quickly left for the hospital. That night after she ate some of the leftover ravioli from her and Matt's lunch, Julie took a bath and crawled into bed. She took her cell phone with her that had all the photos that she had taken of the old plantation. She was trying to imagine back in time living in the house with all of its splendor. Sadly there were living quarters on the property that were probably for the slaves. What a terrible time in our American history to think that people actually owned other people and would force them to do labor on their farms. She wondered what kind of people lived in the big house. Probably just like other slave owners who didn't think it was wrong to own people. It wasn't long before Julie fell asleep thinking about the old house, but more importantly, she was thinking about pastor Matt.

Verses

Chapter 6

Julie woke up to rain pelting on her bedroom window and she thought what a gloomy summer day it was going to be. Although if Matt stopped by the shop it wouldn't be that gloomy at all, but very enjoyable to say the least. On that thought she fixed her breakfast of yogurt and banana, quickly got dressed, and then grabbed her umbrella and hurried out to her car.

Even though it was still raining and it didn't seem like it was ever going to stop, people still came into her store. They were probably looking for something to read and curl up with on the sofa. Mrs. Clayborn came in and bought two more romance novels and a gentleman looking for antique books came in, and Julie quickly removed the old Bible that was sitting on her counter. She took it to the backroom so he wouldn't see it. There were three more customers that just wanted to browse and unfortunately they didn't buy anything. After the lunch hour Julie made a few more sales and several more browsers stopped by. Then a little after four o'clock she got a surprise visit from the pastor.

"Glad I caught you before you closed, I have something I know you're going to like." Matt said as he smiled at Julie and brushed the rain drops off his arms.

"And what might that be Mr. Lewiston?" Julie replied with a flirtatious smile.

"Come on you know my name."

"I most certainly do Mr. Lewiston." Julie snickered and Matt shook his head.

"I went to the courthouse this morning and made a visit to the tax office. I asked the clerk there to look up the tax records on the house on Dry Creek Road. She said that the house was built in 1841 and the original owner's name was Arthur James Williamson. The original description of the house is as follows; as Matt referred to his notes, the property consists of a plantation house, a barn, three slave quarters and four hundred acres of land. The land was used for planting cotton and tobacco. According to the tax records, the taxes are paid each year by a person who lives in the

Raleigh Durham area. The name on the current deed is, Oliver B. Stanton. I guess this sort of thing happens more often than you think the clerk at the courthouse told me. People own property that they don't even know where it's located. I also visited the local Library and looked up information on plantations in the south. Did you know that most plantations were owned by the rich, refined gentlemen that came from England?"

"No, I did not know that."

"Most plantation owners would hire an overseer to be in charge of their slaves. Many times the overseers would be lower class men that would use extremely harsh punishment on the slaves. While their masters would live in big plantation houses, the slaves would live in small log cabins with dirt floors. The slaves would work as many as eighteen hours a day in grueling hot temperatures in the fields and many of them would go to their grave from exhaustion."

"Excuse my language Preacher, but it had to be pure hell for the slaves." Julie said with part anger and sadness in her voice.

"I agree, and please call me Matt, Preacher makes me sound like a man of the cloth in an old western movie."

"Can't picture you with a cowboy hat, but then again, might be kind of interesting."

"I will definitely keep that in mind."

"So, is it possible that we can go back to the house with the clues we found in the old Bible? If there isn't an owner living nearby, then there isn't anyone we can ask to go exploring on the property, so why not?"

"I guess we can. I would like to do a little exploring myself but I'm still not comfortable with it."

"If someone stops us we could always say we got lost while we were hiking." Julie replied with raised eyebrows.

"Wouldn't that be a little dishonest?"

"Not if we're wearing backpacks Pastor."

"You know, my brother Scott is a renowned professional photographer, and he carries his camera everywhere he goes. He's always said,

"You never know when an opportunity for a perfect photo will present itself." I have a camera and I'll bring it along and we'll look like we're getting in some really cool nature shots. So when can we go? Matt asked while looking at his watch.

"I can't go right now, I still have a bookstore to run silly and besides, it's raining, and I'm sure you have some Pastor duties to tend to."

"I'm free on Friday morning, that is, if you can get away then."

"I guess I could keep the store closed until one o'clock on Friday, but then I'll need to reopen, since I'm usually open on Friday nights until eight o'clock."

"Great, I'll meet you here or would you prefer that I pick you up at your place?"

"I'll give you my address, that way, someone won't see my car parked by the store and think that I am open."

"Sounds good, I'll pick you up say around 7:30 Friday morning, and do you mind if I bring my dog Sam along? He could use the exercise."

"Oh please do I love dogs.

Verses

Chapter 7

Julie was ready and waiting outside her apartment when Matt pulled up with a passenger sitting on the seat next to him. When Julie opened the car door Sam, Matt's dog, quickly jumped into the back seat but not until he gave Julie a big sloppy kiss on the face.

"My you have a friendly dog." Julie said as she reached back and gave Sam a loving pat on the head.

"Yea, he's really a laid back dog. If someone tried to rob me he would just lick them to death and maybe even help them haul my stuff away."

"He really doesn't mean that Sam." Julie said as she gave Sam a little hug.

"Oh yes he does." Matt responded with a half laugh.

It was a peaceful and quiet ride out into the country with the early morning North Carolina sun shining as bright as usual. Matt and Julie turned onto Dry Creek Road and it wasn't long before they found the place where they had parked the car when they were there before. Matt hooked Sam to his leash and he and Julie put their backpacks on. The backpacks were almost empty except for a few water bottles and a water bowl for Sam. If someone would stop them they wanted to give the impression that they were hikers.

Matt quickly remembered the path that he and Julie had taken before and it wasn't long before the old plantation house sprouted up in front of them. Sam was having a lot of fun doing what dogs do best, smelling and rooting around the tall grass that seemed to be everywhere. Matt retrieved his camera and took a few pictures of the house and the surrounding area. He thought about his brother Scott who would tromp through the woods for hours trying to capture that perfect picture of anything that moved or whatever he thought would be a good photo. Matt had a whole new respect for his brother's photography business. He and Sam walked backed to the remnants of the log houses and there was no doubt that they were used to house the slaves. He took pictures of the log houses too.

Julie stood for a long time taking in the immense structure of the house. She thought about all the activities that probably went on in and around the house many years ago. She tried not to think about the slaves and the horrors that they must have endured but it was on her mind, and no matter how she tried to make it go away, it was there. The slave's homes, if you could call them that, were nothing but shacks, while the plantation owner and his family enjoyed living in an elegant home from that time period.

Matt and Sam joined Julie and they walked to the front of the house. Matt being much taller than Julie, peeked into one of the front windows.

"Minus the furniture it's like time stood still in there."

"Can I take a peek?" Julie quickly asked.

"Sure but you'll need a boost. Let me help you."

Matt put his hands together and helped Julie so that she could see into the darken interior of the house. She saw that there were a couple pieces of furniture, but on the whole, the house was basically empty.

"Let's go in Matt."

"I don't know about that, what if someone comes along, wouldn't we be breaking and entering?"

"Come on Preacher, where's your sense of adventure?"

"I'd like to go in too Julie but my better judgment says keep out."

"Well you can keep company with your better judgment I'm going in."

Julie tried the front door and after a couple of twists on the old rusty door knob, it gave way, and the door creaked open. Matt and Sam joined her and they were standing in the entrance of the house and facing an enormous stairway that led to the upper part of the house. There was a huge stone fireplace in the living room and a couple of the stones had come loose and fallen out onto the floor. The wood floors were dust covered and in some places the floor boards were a little questionable. Matt tried his weight on some of the boards and they seemed sturdy enough. The doors to some of the rooms were intact but then there were a few doors that were lying on the floor. There was an old wood chair but both of the front legs were broke.

Matt and Sam went into the back of the house which was probably the kitchen area. The original wooden wash sink was still intact, but just about everything else except for piles of leaves and debris that had blown in through a broken windowpane, was long gone. Matt heard Julie call him and he and Sam hurried to see what it was she wanted.

"I'm up here Matt, come on up, the steps on the stairs are safe except for one that's missing, watch out for that one though." Julie warned.

"You're crazy, you could have fallen through the stairs to who knows what below."

"But I didn't, so hurry up, there's more to see up here." Julie said as she disappeared around the corner.

"With our luck Sam, we'll be the ones to fall through the stairs." Matt whispered to his dog.

Matt and Sam nervously but carefully went up the stairs to look for Julie. They found her in one of the many bedrooms just staring and looking intently at something.

"What is it?" Matt wanted to know as he looked around the room that looked at one time to be a child's room and saw something in the corner.

"It's the only thing left in the room and I think it's an old rocking horse. It looks as though it's broken but the horse part is still in one piece. I think it was homemade too because there's straw coming out of one side of the horse. It's hard to believe that a child played with this at one time."

"I had a rocking horse when I was a boy, but it was made of plastic and I had a cowboy hat to go with it." Matt said with a big smile.

"Oh so we're back to that cowboy hat thing."

"I just might have to dig one up just for you." Matt replied.

"You just do that.

Julie looked around the room and she saw some tall cupboards but the doors and hinges were missing except for a lower cupboard that miraculously still had its door attached. The cupboard was close to the floor and out of curiosity she looked inside. It was dark in the cupboard so she used Matt's handy flashlight, and as she shined it inside, she saw something looking back at her that was stuffed in the back. When she realized that it was an old porcelain doll she reached for it and pulled it out of the cupboard. The head was cracked and the doll was missing an eye, one leg and two arms. It was very sooty and dirty from being in the cupboard for a long time. She examined the doll closely with the flashlight and on the back of the doll's head there were numbers and the words, "Made in Germany."

"Look Matt, it's an old porcelain doll must've belonged to a little girl that lived here. I sure wish we could find out more about the family that had originally owned this house. The mystery of it all is killing me. I believe that whoever lived here probably owned that old Bible and one of the members of the family wrote those scriptures in the back of it. But I wonder what they were trying to tell us?"

"We may never know Julie."

"Think about it Matt, the clues in the Bible led us this far, we just can't give up, there has to be more."

"Maybe some other time I think we've explored enough for one day. We should get back to the car this place is starting to give me the creeps."

"All right you win Preacher but I'm not done with this yet."

"I was afraid of that. Come on Sam lets head back to the car."

"I'm right behind you." Julie said as she quickly put the old doll back in the cupboard and followed Matt. As much as she would have liked to examine the doll a little more she would never remove anything from someone's property. It belongs to whoever the owner might be, and the doll should stay with the house, no matter what. It would be like stealing to take something that didn't belong to you, even though it came from a deserted old house, it just wouldn't be right.

Verses

Chapter 8

It had been three days since Julie and Matt visited the old plantation house. The bookstore was busy as usual. People would stop in to pick up some used paperbacks to take on their vacation or just to read on a lazy summer day. Mrs. Clayborn came in to donate some of her romance novels that she had read and passed around to all of her friends. She also picked up some more books to take with her. Matt had called and said he was busy preparing a sermon for next Sunday's service, but wanted to set up a dinner date for next Thursday night. He hoped that she would accept.

Julie was ecstatic and said, "Absolutely Preacher, what time you picking me up?"

Julie couldn't get over finding the broken rocking horse and doll head that belonged to children from the nineteenth century. She thought she would take the time to go over the clues again that were in the old Bible just in case she might have missed something the first go around. When she checked the front of the Bible, she remembered the folded pages that had been tucked inside and had come loose from the binding. She carefully unfolded each page and on the third page she noticed right away another handwritten verse.

The verse was Acts 16:14. She went to the contents page and looked up the page number for the book of Acts. Then she looked up on her computer the Roman numeral converter so that she could find chapter 16. She turned the big pages of the Bible until she found the right page number. She went to chapter XVI which was 16 in Roman numerals and then to verse 14. She spotted right away, the name "Lydia" that was circled in the verse. She read the whole verse that said, "And a certain woman named Lydia, a seller of purple, of the city of Thyatira, which worshipped God, heard us: whose heart the Lord opened, that she attended unto the things which were spoken of Paul." Julie was excited because it was very possible that Lydia was the person that had circled all the other verses that were in the back of the Bible.

    Julie did something that she had never done before. She closed her shop at noon and posted a sign on the door that read, Gone to lunch, be back at one o'clock. She locked the front door and ran the block and a half to the local library. She asked the librarian how she could look up records of a family that had lived near their town of Warrenton back in the 1800's. The librarian had never had a request quite like that before.

The librarian said she could bring Julie some books on the history of the town and maybe that might help her. Julie thought she would give it a try, and who knows, maybe she would find more clues about the old house on Dry Creek Road.

Reading the early history of the town of Warrenton, in two different books, Julie found a reference about the Arthur James Williamson estate. It said that the plantation was one of the oldest plantations in the area and it was built in 1841. This was the information that Matt had gotten from the clerk's office that he told Julie about. There was no more mention about the estate. She wondered what happened to the Williamson family and especially the girl named Lydia. There was only one thing Julie knew she had to do. She had to go back to the plantation house and try to figure out what all those clues meant.

At seven o'clock sharp Matt knocked on Julie's apartment door. She waited for a couple more knocks before she opened the door. She didn't want him to think she was standing on the other side of the door waiting, which she was.

"Nice place you have, I like the vintage furniture."

"It's called vintage Goodwill."

"I was always blessed to have had church parsonages to live in complete with furniture." Matt replied pointing and looking up at the ceiling and he said, thanks. "Although I've been saving for my own place someday."

"When my father passed away, he left me some money and I used it to start my own business and what was left I purchased some necessities. Secondhand furniture works fine for me."

"Ready? I have reservations at the best restaurant in town."

"Since we only have one restaurant I'm guessing its Pete's."

"Your right about Pete's, it is the only restaurant in town, unless you count Nora's Pizza Parlor, but I picked Pete's." Matt said with a smile.

"You are a character." Julie replied.

"I thought I was a cowboy."

"Not unless you're wearing a cowboy hat and I'm not seeing one."

When Julie and Matt arrived at Pete's restaurant, there was only one other table being served and it looked as though that couple was leaving soon. The five o'clock crowd had long departed so that left Julie and Matt with the restaurant all to themselves. Julie told Matt about the verse in the old Bible which she had found and the name "Lydia" in the verse. She also talked about her trip to the library and finding the same information that he had told her about earlier. That the house was built in 1841 and owned by Arthur James Williamson. Julie told Matt that because the Bible was dated 1849, there was a big possibility that the Bible belonged to the Williamson family, and that Lydia was either the wife or a daughter. Matt said that he would try the clerk's office again and see if he could come up with some more information. They finished the special of the day dinner of meatloaf, mashed potatoes and the vegetable of the day, carrots. Then Matt took Julie back to her apartment.

"Thanks Matt, it was a really nice dinner and I really do appreciate it."

"Sorry it wasn't that fancy especially when they put a bottle of catsup in front of your plate."

"It was fancy to me haven't been to a restaurant in a long time."

"I think we should make this a habit, I'd like to do this again real soon Julie." Matt said as he leaned forward and lightly kissed Julie on the lips.

Julie who was caught off guard said, "Sounds like a plan Preacher."

Verses

Chapter 9

Just before Julie arrived at her bookstore her cell phone rang. It was her mother calling probably to see what she was up to. Julie didn't mind her mother calling her, but usually the conversations lasted for at least an hour, and Julie had so much to do when she would open up her store.

"Hello Mother how are you doing? And how's the weather in Philly?"

"Great, the sun is shining and I have a planned luncheon date today with my friends from my Bridge Club. How are you darling meet any handsome men lately?"

"As a matter of fact I have mother." As soon as Julie said it she bit her tongue and wished she could take it back.

"Oh my God when did this happen?"

"He's the new pastor at one of our churches in town. His name is Matthew Lewiston." Julie was thinking to herself this will definitely give her mother something to talk about to her friends at lunch.

"Did you say he was a priest?"

"No Mother, I said he was a pastor not a priest. He's really nice and we've already been on a dinner date."

"Oh please do tell me all about it. I want to know all the details."

"I can't right now Mother, I just pulled up to the bookstore, I'll call you back as soon as I can and fill you in on all the details, I promise."

Julie was glad she didn't have to go into detail about her and Matt. Her mother would want to know everything down to what they ordered for dinner and what did Matt's father do for a living.

It rained during the night so the sidewalk in front of Julie's store was still wet. Her front store windows were spotted from the rain so that meant that she would have to make the extra time to clean her windows. Pioneer Days were next week and she wanted her store to look its best for the festivities. Pioneer Days came only once a year in Warrenton with lots of pig pulling and barbeque chicken on the grill. People came from all over the state to enjoy the craft displays, local rodeo and lots and lots of fun food to eat. Julie planned on having a display of books for sale in front of her store along with a table displaying homemade fancy bookmarkers that her neighbor Connie made. Connie is handicapped and confined to a wheelchair but she gets around easy enough and she even drives her own handicapped van. She would spend her days making lots of craft items for her church and for other benefits. It was always her bookmarkers that were a big success at Julie's store. It gave Connie the extra cash to buy the supplies she needed for all her other crafts. Julie was looking forward to Pioneer Days and she hoped that the weather would cooperate on that much anticipated day.

   While she was daydreaming and reliving her date with Matt, Julie cleaned her store windows. She was hoping he would stop in the store to see her. Before Julie could finish her windows, and put away her cleaning supplies, Mrs. Clayborn came into the store. She always came in on Mondays after running out of books on the weekend.

"Good morning my dear Julie, how are you today?" Mrs. Clayborn cheerfully asked.

"I am just fine Mrs. Clayborn, how can I help you?"

"Oh I'm just looking for a few more interesting books to read."

"I got a few new ones in the store recently that I'm sure you would enjoy." Julie responded knowing full well that Mrs. Clayborn only reads steamy romance novels.

"Please set them aside for me dear but I'm still going to do a little browsing."

"Let me know if you need anything."

Julie put her cleaning stuff away in her back room, and when she returned, Matt was standing in front of her counter.

"I see you recovered from our meatloaf special."

"It was really quite good, it's not often I can enjoy a little home cooking."

"Glad to oblige."

"Hey how would you like to go back to the old house with me?" Julie asked.

"Are you sure you want to go back there?"

"Absolutely. I'm itching to solve the mystery about that house." Julie replied hoping the Pastor would feel the same as she did.

"I'll tell you what. Let's go over the clues again, and who knows, we might even find something to add to our mystery house. After we do that I'll be more than willing to go exploring with you."

"All right, agreed. I have one customer in the store right now, so if you have the time, I can bring the old Bible out and we can get started."

"Whoa, I didn't mean right now." I have to get back to the church to work on church stuff with the church secretary for Sunday's service. I just wanted to stop by and say hello."

"I'm sorry, I understand, I really do. It's just that it's on my mind constantly and I can't think of anything else."

"How about dinner this Friday night? Maybe this time we can try Nora's Pizza Parlor and then we can work on the Bible clues." Matt quickly asked.

"Sounds great, but remember I stay open until eight o'clock on Friday nights, so dinner might be a little late."

"I'm pretty sure Nora's stays open until midnight on Fridays so we'll be ok."

"Well hopefully we won't be out that late. Maybe after dinner we can come back to my store and see if we can find more clues in the Bible. I couldn't very well carry the old Bible to the Pizza Parlor without getting a hernia."

"Sounds good to me." Matt replied as he hurried out the door.

Verses

Chapter 10

   Julie knew she couldn't wait until Friday night for her and Matt to look for more clues in the 1849 Bible. After Mrs. Clayborn left the store with a tote bag full of romance paperbacks, Julie brought the big Bible from the back room and laid it caringly on the counter. She went over the fifteen verses once again that were on the inside back cover of the Bible and after checking her notes, the verses distinctly spelled out, "our dry creek road." The next three verses, which had the words, "steps," "Thou art my hiding- place," and the words, "shut up" and 'be revealed" had also been circled. Julie then remembered where she had found the verse with the name "Lydia." It was found on one of the folded pages that had come separated from the binding and it was in the front of the Bible. So she opened to the front of the Bible and she carefully unfolded more of the loose pages. It didn't take long before she found four more handwritten verses that were on the last folded page that had been tucked neatly into the front of the Bible. The verses were, Hebrews 2:7, Psalm 24:7, John 20:25, and Revelation 20:12. After finding the book of Hebrews from the Bible's Contents page, and pulling up on her computer the Roman numeral converter in case she needed it, Julie looked up Hebrews 2:7. The verse read, "Thou madest him a little lower than the angels; thou crownedst him with glory and honour, and didst set him over the works of thy hands." And the word "lower" was circled. She then turned to Psalm 24:7 and the verse read, "Lift up your heads, O ye gates; and be ye lift up, ye everlasting doors; and the King of glory shall come in." The word "door" without the s was circled. Next was John 20:25 and that verse read as follows, "The other disciples therefore said unto him, We have seen the Lord. But he said unto them, Except I shall see in his hands the print of the nails, and put my finger into the print of the nails, and thrust my hand into his side, I will not believe." The words "the print of the nails" was circled. The last verse was Revelation 20:12, and that verse read, "And I saw the dead, small and great, stand before God, and the books were opened: and another book was opened, which is the book of life; and the dead were judged out of those things which were written in the books, according to their works." The words, "the book of life" were circled.

"Oh my," Julie said out loud as she looked at the words that were circled that she had written down on her notepad. She compared the words with the words from the first set of verses that she and Matt had figured out and she put them all together. In order, all the words came out like this, "our dry creek road," "steps," "Thou art my hiding place," "shut up" and "be revealed," "lower," "door," "the print of the nails," and finally, "the book of life." Then she added the special verse that she found with the name "Lydia" circled. Julie's heart was fluttering and she was positive that Lydia was trying to tell her something through the many clues from the verses in the 1849 Bible. There was no question, she had to go back to the old house, and she knew she couldn't wait until after Friday to go.

Julie quickly went over her schedule, and because Tuesday's were usually not as busy as the other days of the week, she decided to close on Tuesday and go exploring. She knew that the rest of the week she would be tied up getting ready for Pioneer days.

Julie carefully put the old Bible back on the shelf in her storeroom. When she came back to the front of the store, Connie had pulled up in her handicapped van. Julie held the door open for Connie to come into the store in her wheelchair. She had a full box of bookmarkers that she had made especially for Pioneer Days. Julie was always in wonder as she ran her finger over the delicate work that Connie had put into each of her bookmarkers. While praising Connie on the colors she had chosen, it came to Julie to show Connie the bookmarker which she had found in the old Bible. When Connie saw the bookmarker she was fascinated with the intricate and delicate crochet work. Right away she asked Julie where she had found it. When Julie said she found the bookmarker in an old Bible dated 1849 Connie was not surprised. She said that the work looked like the kind of work you would expect from that time period. Julie wanted desperately to tell her friend about her adventure to the old house, and about the Bible, but she decided to wait until she had definite proof that the Bible and the plantation house were related.

After Connie left the store Julie's cell phone rang, and before she saw who was calling, she already knew it was her mother.

"Hello Mother, how are you today?" Julie cringed waiting for her mother's reply only because she knew her mother would have lots of questions for her.

"I'm fine Julie but how are you and that priest you're dating?"

"I told you mother, he's a pastor not a priest."

"So what's the difference?

"There is a difference Mother, a priest is an ordained priest for the Catholic Church, and a pastor or minister is usually one who presides over other Christian Churches.

"Like I said, no difference."

"Never mind Mother, how's your weather?"

"Great, now tell me more about this man. I want to know every detail."

"We only went on one date Mother, he is very nice, and we're going out again this Friday night."

"Oh I am so thrilled for you dear, where is he taking you? A nice place I hope."

"It's called, Nora's Pizza Parlor Mom, one of only two places in town to eat."

"How dreadful, you sure there isn't somewhere else he could take you?"

"I'm sure Mother, besides, I love pizza you know that. Mom, I have a customer coming into the store, I have to go, talk to you later, bye, love you." And Julie quickly hung up before she could hear her mother say the word but.

Verses

Chapter 11

Julie was excited and she hoped that when she closed the store early, no one would come into the store so she could get an early start. She put the closed sign in the front window and quickly locked things up and hurried to her car. It was a pleasant sunny day and she had lots of hours of daylight to go on her adventure. As she was driving down the road she went over again in her head the Bible clues. The first fifteen verses in the back of the Bible spelled out "our dry creek road." The road where she and Matt found the old house. The next three verses had the words, "steps," "Thou art my hiding- place," and "shut up" and "be revealed." The four circled verses that Julie just recently found were, "lower," "door," "the print of the nails" and "the book of life."

Julie pulled onto Dry Creek Road and she slowed down until she came to the place where the abandoned house entrance was located and she parked her car. It was a good thing she had changed shoes and put on her hiking boots, because the recent rain had made the old dirt path somewhat muddy. She had her notepad with her, which had all the clues from the Bible, and she was more than ready to figure out what the clues in the Bible were trying to tell her. As she continued on the path to the house, without Matt, she had to push away the briars, thickets and overgrown weeds all by herself. As predicted, the house hadn't changed a bit. The weathered and rundown look of the house was sad and hard for Julie to comprehend. She stood for a long time looking at the house and listening for any sounds. The only sound was the sound of a slight breeze that was sweeping through the tall grass. Julie had a feeling that the old house was actually glad to see her. Even the windows seemed to smile back at her in an eerie kind of way. She jiggled the rusty lock and the door opened just as it did when she and Matt were there before. Julie's heart was beating wildly as she realized that she didn't have the protection of Matt and Sam beside her. She took a deep breath, and as she went into the house, she found herself staring once again at the massive staircase. Instantly she remembered one of the clues in the Bible which was "steps." She went up the stairs stepping over the missing step and continued on to the upper rooms. She went into each room and explored but at the same time wondered about the family that had lived there. She checked her notes and the next clues were "Thou art my hiding- place" and "shut up" and "be revealed." She looked around in each room but couldn't find anything that would be a hiding place. Most old houses didn't have closets to put their clothes in, they would use an armoire or something similar to for their clothes. So other than windows and fireplaces Julie didn't see any hiding places. As she went back into what she thought would have been a child's room, Julie remembered the cupboard and it quickly came to her that the next clues she had written on her notepad were, "lower" and "door." She hoped the clues were in reference to the low cupboard door. She opened the door and thank goodness she had remembered to bring a flashlight with her. She shined the light into the cupboard and right away saw the cracked porcelain doll that she had found before. She carefully placed the broken doll outside the cupboard and she looked at her notes again and saw the clue, "the print of the nails." She shined the flashlight around the inside of the cupboard but it was totally empty. She just couldn't figure out the next clue. Then as she shined the light on the wood floor boards in the cupboard there was one board in particular that had more than one nail to hold it down. In fact there were at least six nails holding the board in place and they were all in a circle on the board. None of the other boards had that many nails in them. Julie thought, this must be what Lydia was trying to say from the verse, "the print of the nails." Julie didn't have any kind of tool with her so she looked around the room to see if there was something she could use to lift the board. She spied the old rocking horse and quickly went over and found one of the splintered rockers lying next to the horse and she picked it up. Just then something made a loud bang, and she dropped the piece of wood and stood silently, too scared to move an inch. She listened to the point that she could actually hear her heartbeat. Then she heard another sound and she swore it was a door closing. That did it, Julie quickly closed the cupboard door and she tried to walk quietly on the old wooden floors, but they just squeaked too much. She was now scared out of her mind and every kind of vision and thought was entering her head. When she got to the bottom of the stairs, she saw that the door she had left open was now closed. She told herself that it could have been the wind, but maybe it wasn't. As fast as she could she left the house and literally ran down the path to return to her car. She didn't take a deep breath until she was safely on the highway and heading back home.

Verses

Chapter 12

It was just before five o'clock and Julie thought by chance Matt might still be working in his office at the church. If he was, she was going to talk to him about the Bible verses and especially about her scary trip back to the old house. She knew that he would be upset that she had gone there without him. Luckily, when she went inside the church, she found Matt busy in his office and probably working on a new sermon.

"Nice church you have here Preacher." Julie said with a grin as she noticed that Matt's dog Sam was sleeping under his desk. Sam woke up when he heard Julie's voice and he wagged his tail as he came over to see her.

"Well, what brings you to God's house?"

"Need to talk to you about something. I went back to the old house today to try to solve a few clues." Julie said as Sam laid down beside her chair and she began stroking his fur.

"You didn't."

"Yea I did. I know I should have waited for you Matt, but I just couldn't, I had to go back and see if there was something that I missed when we were there before."

"Well Indiana Jones, what did you find?"

"You know how the first fifteen verses led us to "our dry creek road," well, I'm pretty sure I solved the next three verses that we found on the back cover." Julie continued as she looked at her notes. "The clues in the three verses are, "steps," "Thou art my hiding- place," and "shut up" and "be revealed." I'm positive these verses describe the inside of the house."

"How do you know that?" Matt asked as he sat back in his leather chair and listened intently to Julie talk about the mystery of the old house. He liked Julie a lot and he found himself thinking about her most of the time. Even though she wasn't a church goer, he thought in time, he might be able to sway her to come to church with him.

"I took my notes with me when I went into the old house and it came to me when I looked at the old staircase. I remembered the circled word "steps." and I figured it was in reference to the staircase, so I went back upstairs. I ventured from room to room but I couldn't find anything until I remembered the cupboard in the room which you and I found. The clues "Thou art my hiding-place," and "shut up" and "be revealed," would describe the cupboard perfectly. Then the next four clues," and before Julie could finish Matt quickly interrupted her.

"What next four clues are you talking about?"

"Oh, I forgot to tell you. Along with the name "Lydia," in the verse that I had told you about, I also found four more verses that were on pages that had also been folded in the front of the Bible. I looked up those verses and wrote down the circled words."

"Wait, you looked up the verses?"

"Well, probably not as fast as you would have. The Roman numeral chapters slowed me down a bit. But with the help of the Roman numeral converter on my computer, in time, I was able to figure all of them out. Anyways, the circled clues in those verses were, "lower," "door," "the print of the nails," and "the book of life."

"I'm impressed." Matt said with fascination and Julie continued.

"So, the clues "lower" and "door" would apply to the lower cupboard that has a door. I searched inside the cupboard with my flashlight, and other than the broken porcelain doll, I couldn't find anything more."

"I take it you came to a dead end."

"No, I actually found one of the floor boards that had a circle of nails that were holding the board in place. I believe that the multiple nailed board would be in reference to the clue, "the print of the nails." I was in the process of looking for something to lift the board up when I head the door downstairs close and it nearly gave me a heart attack." Reliving it all over again, Julie was shaking a little and Matt's dog Sam sensed that she was upset and he got up quickly and licked her hand to let her know that everything was alright.

"You really are brave. I would have jumped out of my skin."

"I did run out of there as fast as I could. Sad part of it is, I didn't get a chance to see what was underneath that board."

"Promise me something? That you won't go back there again without me, and I'm not going back until I do more research on the current owner. That way we can ask permission to be on his property."

"I promise I won't go back without you, but please hurry with that research, I'd like to get back to the house as soon as possible. It's killing me to know what's under that board."

"Let's put all that aside for now and while you're here, If you don't mind, I would like to give you a little tour and show you our beautiful church."

The first thing Matt showed Julie was the big sanctuary with the tall wooden cross that was highlighted with lights that were hidden behind it. He showed her his podium where he gave his Sunday sermons. He then took her for a tour and showed her all the classrooms from the nursery on up to the adult class. He said if she was free next Sunday he would love for her to come and listen to one of his sermons. She thanked him for the invitation and said she would definitely give it some thought.

Before Julie left the church, Matt reminded her about their date on Friday night. She said she hadn't forgotten and she was really looking forward to it. She left the church with a wonderful feeling of comfort, not only from spending time with Matt, but from being inside the church. In her heart she was already planning to go to church on Sunday and hear Matt talk about God.

Verses

Chapter 13

It was Friday and Julie was more than ready for Pioneer Days next week in Warrenton. Julie worked hard all week just getting ready for it. She had a new supply of used books in her store inventory and she had ordered some new books to place in her front window along with a few collectible antique books. She had Connie's beautiful bookmarkers on a table adjacent to her store counter and everything in her store was clean and ready for Pioneer Days customers.

After Julie closed her shop Friday night, she was tired, but more than ready and to go out with Matt and have something warm and sinful to eat. On her way home she called her mother.

"Hi Mom, just wanted you to know how my week went getting ready for Pioneer Days. I'm hoping to get some new customers and sell a lot more books."

"I'm really happy for you dear, I always knew you would do well with your own bookstore. Are you still going out tonight with that priest?"

"Pastor Mother and yes we're still going to the pizza parlor. I'm also going to go to his church on Sunday."

"Well that's nice."

Julie could tell that her mother was a little uncomfortable talking about church. She didn't want to make her mother feel bad so she dropped the subject.

"I'm home now Mother, I need to quickly get ready for my date tonight but I'll give you a call this weekend and let you know how it went."

"You be sure to do that dear and say hi to the priest for me."

"I will, and I love you too Mother."

Since she was running late, Julie phoned Matt and told him that she would meet him at the pizza parlor to save time. When she arrived, Nora's smelled heavenly with the smell of pizza as she walked inside the door. Julie didn't care that it wasn't a four star restaurant, she just wanted to enjoy some hot pizza.

"How was work today?" Matt asked as he handed Julie a menu as she sat down."

"Great, made more sales than usual."

"Sorry but there's not that many items on the menu to pick from but what's there, trust me, is really good."

"I do trust you Matt and whatever you order I'll eat I'm starved."

"Ok I'll do the ordering and I'm pretty sure you're going to like it."

"Sounds good. Did you have a chance to do some research on the current owner of the old house?"

"Just that he lives in Raleigh, I'm thinking that if I can track him down, and after telling him about our research of the family that lived there, he might give us permission to be on his property."

"That doesn't help us any right now. I really want to go back to the house and see what's under that floor board. I understand we need the approval of the owner first, but can't we sneak in just one more time? Come on, what do you say Preacher, up to another adventure?"

"You do have me curious about what's under that board, but I'm really afraid we're going to get shot for trespassing. It is someone else's property you know."

"Just one more trip and I promise I won't go back again until we have permission." Julie replied as she bit into a piece of pizza that was loaded and dripping with mozzarella cheese.

"I'll tell you what, you come to church on Sunday to hear one of my sermons and I promise I'll go back with you to the old house."

"You got yourself a deal." Julie said knowing full well that she had already planned to go to Matt's church on Sunday.

Julie put on her best black and white stripped dress and black heels and she was on her way to the Church of Christ. She was pleasantly welcomed at the door by several nice people and they handed her a church bulletin. She took a seat two rows up from the back of the church. She sang with the congregation, some songs she knew, but many she had never heard of before. When Matt took the podium, she felt a sense of pride as he greeted the congregation and gave an opening prayer. His sermon was good, no it was wonderful, and Julie was glad that she had agreed to come. After church Matt shook hands with people in line that were leaving the church. When he reached to shake hands with Julie, he held onto her hand a little longer then he did with anyone else. She squeezed his hand back and said, "Nice sermon Preacher." Julie knew that Matt had his usual Sunday duties to tend to so she didn't bother him the rest of the day. But she did message him on his cell phone to say she enjoyed the experience and thanked him for inviting her to the Church of Christ.

Verses

Chapter 14

Connie arrived early at Julie's bookstore to get ready for the first day of Pioneer Days in Warrenton. It was a beautiful day and the weather was cooperating so far. Several businesses had their merchandise sitting on the sidewalks in front of their stores for customer convenience. Barbeque grills and smokers were set up on the far end of town and the smells were intoxicating from the chicken, pork and beef that had probably been cooking since daybreak. There were several canvas tents set up on Main Street for crafts and photographers and painters to display their wares. Already people started milling through the streets to get ahead of the anticipated crowd. Julie tied balloons to two of her planters that sat in the front of her store and she did some last minute tidying up before the first customer came through the door.

The first day of Pioneer Days went extremely well with lots of sales, and on the second day, Julie did even better. Connie sold all her bookmarkers by the middle of the week, and all in all, it was a successful event. Matt stopped in to visit towards the end and told Julie he would be free on Monday if she wanted to venture out to the old house. She said she would close her store until one o'clock that day and they could go first thing that morning.

Julie arrived early at her bookstore on Monday so that she could put her work clothes in the storeroom for when she got back from hiking through the woods. This way she would have clean clothes to put on for work. Matt arrived on time and they were off on another adventure. Julie reminded Matt on the way that she had only one more clue left to solve. It was Revelation 20:12, and the words in the verse, "the book of life" had been circled. They neither one had any idea what the clue meant. But Julie felt that whatever was beneath the floor board would produce the answer.

Matt led the way through the briars and thickets until it opened up to the tall grass growing around the old plantation. Everything was still the same as before and seemingly untouched. There wasn't a breeze so Julie figured that the house would be stiflingly hot, which it was, when they entered through the unlocked front door. Julie wasn't as afraid, as she was the day she hurried out of the house, the last time she was there. She just figured that the wind had pulled the door shut that day. They made their way to the upstairs and to the room with the broken rocking horse. The cupboard door was closed just as Julie had left it and the splintered piece of wood from the rocking horse, which she was going to use to pry the board up, was still lying on the floor beside the cupboard. She didn't need it anyway because this time she brought with her a couple of tools. She pulled out a screwdriver from her pocket and Matt stopped her and said he would do it. He was careful trying not to damage the wood too much and after a couple of tries the board came loose and he lifted it up and laid it on top of the board next to it. Julie shined her flashlight down into the dark space and right away she saw an old tin box. She looked at Matt with raised eyebrows and said, "This ought to be interesting." Matt lifted the tin box out of its hiding place and placed the box outside the cupboard. Using the window nearby for light, he opened the rusty latch on the front of the box, and as he did, little flakes of rust fell to the floor. There was a small leather book inside the box and Julie carefully lifted it out. She was almost afraid to turn the cover.

"I believe it's a diary. That's what the clue, "the book of life" meant Matt, it's a diary."

"Well you have my curiosity now what does it say?" Matt anxiously wanted to know.

"It says." "My name is Lydia Abigail Williamson. Matt, that's the name I found circled in the Bible. Then it says, I was born May 15, 1842 and I have one brother, Jacob Allen Williamson and he was born, September 22, 1844. My mother's name is Mary Allison Thomas Williamson and my father's name is Arthur James Williamson. This diary was given to me by my grandmother, Sarah Isabelle Thomas, for my tenth birthday. It is May 20, 1852, and it has been five days since my birthday. Here I will begin to keep the record of my thoughts and what will happen in my life."

"That's "the book of life" clue Matt, its Lydia's diary of her life."

"I'm sure you're right, what else does it say?"

"She writes, I have not enjoyed Grandmother's visit from the city. She has been good to my brother Jacob but not as much to me, and I don't believe she likes my father very much, they do not converse with each other. My father presented me with a doll from Germany for my birthday and my grandmother told my father that the gift was much too extravagant a gift for a young girl of ten. My father disagreed."

"Wow, it's like going back in time Matt, I can't believe this diary has been hidden in the floor boards for all these years. I wonder if the old porcelain doll was the doll that Lydia was talking about. It did say on the doll's neck, Made in Germany. Do you think it would be wrong of me to take the diary home and study it more closely to find out more about the Williamson house?"

"No, not as long as you put it back when you're done with it. The diary is part of the Williamson estate and it belongs with the house."

"Don't worry Preacher, I'll put it back."

When Matt and Julie went back down the stairs of the old house, and saw that the front door was still wide open, they both figured that it must have been the wind that had shut the door when Julie was there before. They returned to the bookstore and Julie changed her clothes and went to work right away going through the many books that had been deposited in her book drop over the weekend. Matt went to his office at the church to prepare a sermon for next Sunday and go over the information that would be in the church bulletin.

   Julie was exhausted when she finally crawled into bed that night after eating a frozen dinner that she had quickly fixed for herself. She didn't have time to stop at the store and get the stuff to make a salad, and the only thing she had to choose from, was a couple of frozen dinners. She ate her pasta dinner in a hurry because she wanted to read Lydia's diary before she went to bed. She couldn't wait to read what Lydia wrote in her diary way back in the 1800's. It wasn't a daily journal but more of an account of the events that had occurred in Lydia's life. She wrote how her brother suffered a rash all over his body and how he spent two weeks in bed because of it. She wrote about a fire that happened in their kitchen and how furious her father was at the slave named Sadie. Lydia gave an account of each of her birthdays and she mentioned one Christmas which they had such a feast and they even had a dusting of snow on Christmas morning when they woke up. She wrote about the Christmas tree that Joe's cut and brought into the house and they found a bird's nest deep inside the tree. Julie wondered who Joe's was. As Julie continued to read she felt like she was living Lydia's life through her secret diary. Lydia wrote about how her mother showed her how to make a bookmarker like the one her mother had made for the family Bible. Julie wondered if the bookmarker that she found in the old Bible could possibly be the bookmarker that Lydia's mother had made. Lydia told about her cousin Beth who had drowned when crossing the ice on the family pond. There was the usual mention of more birthdays and then Julie read about someone that Lydia referred to as Joe's the Negro boy and how much work he did for her father. Lydia wrote that she liked to talk to him when she played with her brother Jacob on the big porch. She also wrote how Joe's would tell her secrets, and if she told anyone about the secrets, he would be beaten or maybe even die because of it. Joe's told Lydia when the Master Williamson would go away, one of the man slaves would be brought to her mother's bedroom and be there all night.

Julie was stunned, she always knew from reading history accounts of how slave owners would beat and rape the Negro slaves that they owned. The slaves were treated horribly and not how a human being should have been treated. It was just common knowledge during that era that slave masters could do whatever they wanted to the slaves they owned. Julie quickly got out of bed and looked up on her computer what she had never known before. White women would also use their slaves for whatever their purpose. They would sometimes have them beat for no reason but to watch it being done, or even go to bed with them when their husbands were away. It was a social taboo at that time, but it did happen Julie read on the computer.

Lydia wrote in the diary that Joe's was whipped many times and Joe's father had also been whipped. She did not want her friend Joe's to be whipped anymore, so she didn't tell anyone what Joe's had told her. Julie read on and there was an entry in the diary dated July 14, 1853. It said, "My mother gave birth today to a little baby and my father had Joe's come to the house. Joe's told me that my father gave him a baby wrapped in a blanket and he told Joe's, "The baby has died boy, bury it deep in the woods." Then Lydia wrote, Joe's told me that he got a shovel and carried the baby to the woods. Before he buried the baby, he looked under the blanket and saw that the baby was dark like him and he felt real bad that the baby had died. He said before he placed the baby in the grave he named the baby "Angel," because the baby looked like an angel to him. He said that he buried the baby Angel in the woods under the big oak tree next to the old creek. Joe's said he put stones on top of the dirt and he made the stones look like a Jesus cross.

"Oh my God," Julie said to herself. The baby was half African American and half white, and sadly it died, because the baby would have been Lydia's sister.

Julie read on and she read where Joe's showed Lydia where he had buried the baby and Lydia drew a map on one of the pages in her diary to show where the baby was in the ground. Lydia wrote that Joe's father, along with all the other male slaves on the plantation were badly whipped that day. One of the slaves was whipped so bad that he died two days later. Lydia also wrote that Joe's said he couldn't talk to her anymore because he was afraid he would die too. Lydia said she was sad to never be able to see or talk to her friend Joe's again. Julie turned the pages of the diary to get to the end and she saw where Lydia's last words were. "I have hidden this journal of my life in a safe place because no one should read what I have written. Someday when I have gone to my maker in heaven, I hope that someone will find this book through the verses I have circled in the family Bible. Sincerely, Lydia Abigail Williamson."

Well I'll be darn Julie thought, and if I wasn't that person to do just that, over one hundred and sixty years later. It was ten o'clock and Julie hoped that Matt would still be up. She anxiously called him on her cell phone and he answered on the first ring.

"Hi Julie what's up?"

"I just needed to talk to you Matt, am I calling at a bad time?"

"Heck no, me and Sam are having popcorn and watching a baseball game on TV."

"I just finished reading most of Lydia's diary and you won't believe what she wrote." Julie said and then for the next several minutes she told Matt everything she learned from the diary including the part about Lydia's mother having a part African American baby.

"That's amazing, no wonder Lydia kept the diary hidden. If someone would have read that diary, hard telling what would have happened to some of the people she mentioned in it."

"Just the thought that she wanted someone to find it someday with the clues she had left in the 1849 Bible was pretty cool." Julie said as she ran her fingers over the leather cover of the diary. "Lydia was a very smart little girl. She had to have read the Bible from front to back to know where to find the words to circle."

"So now what are you going to do Sherlock?"

"I really like that old house on Dry Creek Road Matt, I think about it all the time and I wonder what it would be like for someone to restore it to its original splendor. When I'm there, I kind of feel like Scarlet in "Gone with The Wind."

"There are similarities between you and Scarlet. If I remember, she was bit feisty and determined just like you." Matt said.

"You're just too funny for words Preacher."

"By the way, what are you doing on Wednesday night?"

"Why do you ask?"

"Because I would like you to come with me to Bible class on Wednesday night. That is if you're free."

"I thought church was on Sundays."

"It is, this is a group that studies the Bible. It's a lot of fun, and you get to meet some of the people from my church. So what do you say, are you in?"

"I guess it couldn't hurt, what time?"

"I'll pick you up around seven, don't eat anything though, we serve pizza on Wednesday nights. Of course it's delivered from Nora's Pizza Parlor." Matt said with a big grin.

"Now I know I'll be there, I love Nora's pizza."

"You are a trip, see you at seven."

Verses

Chapter 15

It's Wednesday and Julie is extremely busy at the bookstore. She has a lot to catch up on after taking the days off exploring the old plantation house. She was just starting to catch up when her mother called.

"How was your date with the priest at the pizza place Julie?"

"I told you before Mother, he is not a priest, he's a pastor."

"Sorry dear, pastor it is, how was your night out?"

"It was great Mom, I'm really liking Matt and I think he likes me too."

"So is this the one Julie? I mean you haven't had much luck with men lately."

"Gee thanks Mom, that's encouraging. Maybe it's because the right one hasn't come along yet. I guess I've been waiting for someone like Matt to come into my life, and yes, I think Matt could be the one."

"Well, hallelujah it's about time."

"Don't get too excited Mom, so far, we've only been on a few dates. As a matter of fact he's picking me up tonight for Wednesday night Bible study at his church."

"That's nice dear, well I have to go, Jan's coming and we're going to the club for lunch today."

"Ok Mom, You have a nice lunch, bye for now."

Julie wished that her mother would get involved with a church, it would do her some good to mingle with women who aren't just thinking about clothes, clubs and what their neighbors are up to.

Matt picked Julie up at her apartment and they were off to Wednesday night Bible study. Julie didn't own a Bible, except for the big 1849 Bible at the bookstore, but she knew that there would be plenty of Bibles at the church. Julie sat quietly as Matt led the discussion group about the book of Revelation. Julie never read the Bible so the complex verses of Revelation were intriguing and fascinating to say the least. She listened as Matt deciphered each of the verses and opened up the lines for discussion. It amazed Julie how the people around her knew so much about the Bible. She felt like a kindergarten kid in a high school class. When it was over, they all had some pizza from Nora's, and later when Matt took her home, she thanked him for taking her and told him she would like to go again sometime. Matt was pleased that Julie enjoyed herself. Before she went inside her apartment, Matt kissed her on the lips and then Julie reached up with both hands and pulled him close and kissed him back passionately.

Before Matt left, Julie made the remark, "I could get used to this Preacher."

"Get used to it." Matt returned smiling.

It had been several weeks since Julie and Matt had been to the old house. It was really bothering Julie having the diary in her possession and she wanted to put it back as soon as possible. It belonged in the old house. Also she wanted to explore the wooded area near the house to see if she could find Angel's grave. Julie and Matt planned a trip on a Monday and Julie closed her shop for the whole day. Matt, Julie and Sam took a ride out to the old house. With their hiking boots and backpacks on, Matt, Julie and with Sam following them, headed for the house. Equipped with the map that Lydia had drawn, they searched the wooded area near the house. They were looking for a big tree by a creek when by chance they came upon an old cemetery that was almost buried. The overgrown weeds and thick brush had clothed the cemetery to a point where you could hardly see it. There were remnants of an old wrought iron gate and a fence that during its era would have been quite impressive. The gate was barely hanging on to its hinges now and it wouldn't budge because of all the vines that had grown up and over it. Matt was able to pull the gate open just enough for the two of them to squeeze through. Julie followed him as he pushed away more vines and brush to expose a tall grave stone that said in great big letters, "Williamson."

"Matt, this must be the Williamson family cemetery."

"I'm pretty sure it is Julie, and along with the big grave stone there are several smaller ones nearby. I don't know about you but I can hardly read the names on some of them. The elements have smoothed their names right off the front of the stones. The only clue is the Williamson name in big letters on the big marker."

"This can't be where Angel is buried, there's not a tree here that's as big as the one Lydia described."

"This wouldn't be where Angel is buried Julie, back then slaves were not buried with their owners family. I did some research on that and most times the slaves were buried away from their owner's cemetery and the only markers they would have, if they even had one, would be just a stone with no markings on it at all."

"That's so sad and so wrong."

"I know but that's what they did back then. Let's look for a creek and then maybe we can find the big tree where Joe's buried the baby under. If it's still there, it would be a very old tree by now. Come on Sam, let's do some more exploring."

Matt, Julie and Sam hiked down an old deer path that narrowed as they walked, but they were determined to keep on going. At the end of the path they found a babbling creek and there next to the creek stood a huge majestic old oak tree with long extending limbs. The tree could easily be well over a hundred and sixty years old. Julie hurried over to the tree and she quickly tried pushing the tall weeds and brush away from the tree. She was having a difficult time, so Matt took over and even Sam did a little digging nearby. After they removed the twigs and dead leaves away from the base of the tree, there in front of them, were fist sized gray stones in the shape of a cross. Julie was overjoyed and then she was overcome with emotion as she ran her hands over the smooth stones in the shape of what Joe's the young slave boy had described as a Jesus cross.

Before they left, Julie and Matt removed most of the foliage and debris away from the stones and then Matt said a nice prayer for little baby Angel. They returned to the house and Julie placed the diary back in its hiding place and she even nailed down the board.

"There, now you're back where you belong, with this old house and all of its secrets and the memory of a little girl named Lydia and a young boy named Joe's that was her friend."

"I know this sounds a little silly Matt, but I feel like there's a part of me that is also being left behind in this house."

"I understand Julie."

Matt and Julie followed Sam, who by now, knew his way on the path back to the car. It was very quiet during the drive but they both had a feeling of great satisfaction as they took their time going back to Warrenton.

Verses

Chapter 16

It had been two months since Julie and Matt had visited the old plantation house with Sam. Julie had been busy with the bookstore and Matt with his duties at the church. They would go out for dinner once a week either at Pete's or at Nora's for pizza. In between Julie would go with Matt to Wednesday night Bible study. One time Julie invited Matt over to her apartment for a Mexican dinner and a movie. It was hard for Matt not to want to stay over, he truly loved Julie and Julie loved him, but they both agreed that they were not ready, and besides, it wouldn't be proper for the new Pastor in town to have a sleepover. But kissing was ok and they sure did a lot of that.

One Sunday after church, Matt told Julie he wanted to take her for a ride out in the country. He told her he would pick her up around two o'clock. When he arrived at her doorstep he was sporting a big black cowboy hat.

"Well I'll be darn, if you don't own a cowboy hat, and a handsome one at that Preacher."

"I aim to please ma'am."

When Matt turned down Dry Creek Road on their little trip Julie was surprised and confused when he stopped where the path led to the old house.

"Why are we here?" Julie quickly asked.

"Just wanted to see the old house one more time." Matt replied.

They followed the path that they both knew so well until it opened up to the grand old house. Matt led the way and up onto the porch, and after he opened the door with a little push, he quickly lifted a surprised Julie up in his arms and carried her over the threshold.

"Gee I feel like Scarlet O'Hara."

"Frankly my dear, I don't give a damn."

"My, oh my, I'll have to wash your mouth out with soap Preacher."

"Just you try."

Matt put Julie down and told her to look on the old wood mantel above the fireplace. Julie hurried over and there laying on the mantel, on top of a little white box, was a beautiful diamond ring. When she turned around Matt was on one knee.

"Julie Devers, will you marry me?"

"You bet I will cowboy." And Julie jumped into Matt's arms and they kissed passionately.

"Now that I'll have myself a new wife, I'll need someplace for her to live." Then Matt produced a piece of paper and handed it to Julie.

"Matt, this is the deed to this house and it's got your name on it!"

"I hate giving my wife a rundown old house, but with a little fixing up, I think we can make it work."

"I can't think of anything I would love more. It's like giving me the Taj Mahal Matt." Julie said with tears in her eyes.

"You might not think that after we start restoring it."

"But I still don't understand Matt, I thought the house belonged to a man living in Raleigh."

"It did, but I've been working on purchasing the house from Mr. Stanton for over a month and a half now. The man said he owns several old houses and he told me he could easily part with one of them."

"I can't believe it. Oh there's so much we can do with this house. It'll be fun restoring it to its natural beauty. Just think, we can put the old Bible and the diary together on a special table after we move in, I just can't wait."

"First things first dear, I think you have a wedding to plan." Matt said with a grin.

"Did I tell you how much I love you Preacher?"

"Not nearly enough."

Verses

Chapter 17

It was a beautiful fall day for the wedding of Julie Devers and Pastor Matthew Lewiston. The sky was a vivid Carolina blue and the leaves on the trees were in brilliant colors of red, orange and yellow. The "Church of Christ" in all of its splendor was decorated with big white bows on the inside as well as on the outside front step rails. The parking lot was full because Matt and Julie had invited the whole church to attend their wedding. Julie's mother brought her best friend all the way from Philadelphia for the wedding. The mother of the bride was wearing a designer made blue dress with a matching big blue hat. The church was full with standing room only in the back. Programs were passed out by the groomsmen and the church organist played the beautiful music that Julie and Matt had picked out especially for their wedding. Julie's mother practically begged Julie to wear a designer dress from a boutique Bridal store in Philadelphia. But instead, Julie had decided to wear a vintage dress and veil that she had found in an antique store in her little town of Warrenton.

The dress had lots of vintage ivory lace and it fit Julie perfectly. Except for the dress needing a good dry cleaning, and a little mending with a stitch here or there, the dress looked as if it were made just for her. Julie's bouquet had white gardenias and she carried a little white Bible that Matt had given her as a wedding gift. Matt was wearing his best Sunday black suit. They both wanted, much to Julie's mother's dismay, to have a no nonsense no frills wedding. They had made a pact to save up all the money they could to pay for the upcoming restoration of their home. Matt's Brother Scott wanted to be the wedding photographer and he didn't charge a thing for the photos as a wedding gift to Matt and Julie. Matt's sister Stephanie, and her husband George and their four children came all the way from Minnesota to share in the big event. Julie asked Stephanie to be one of her bridesmaids, along with Matt's niece Natalie. Julie's best friend Connie was her Maid of Honor. Matt's five year old niece MeeSong, who was adopted from South Korea, was Julie and Matt's little flower girl. Matt's three nephews, Ben, Caleb and Scott's son Nathan were Matt's groomsmen along with his brother Scott who was naturally his best man. The organist played the wedding march and MeeSong in a chiffon pink dress reluctantly at first, but with a little coaching, walked down the church aisle dropping little white flower petals from a small wicker basket. Then came Natalie, Matt's sister Stephanie and Connie, also wearing pink chiffon dresses. Connie's wheelchair was decorated in delicate pink and white flowers. The big surprise to everyone in the church was when Sam, Matt's dog, wearing a black bow tie around his neck also walked down the aisle and then obediently sat at Matt's feet waiting for Julie. Matt, with his groomsmen waited in front of the church for Julie to walk down the aisle. Matt's Pastor and friend from another church proceeded over the ceremony. Not too many people noticed the table sitting under the big wooden cross that was holding the 1849 Bible that brought Matt and Julie together on that fateful day. Julie's mother walked her down the aisle to a proud but emotional groom. When Matt and Julie were pronounced man and wife, they kissed and Caleb, Matt's nephew, let out a whoop and everyone laughed. Instead of renting a place to have the wedding reception, the church ladies got together and gave Matt and Julie a very nice reception in the church's reception hall. Julie's friend Beth, at the Bakery Shop down from her bookstore, donated a triple layer wedding cake. Matt and Julie did not ask for wedding gifts, but if anyone insisted on getting them a gift, a Home Depot gift card would be much appreciated.

Most of the congregation of the church along with Matt and Julie's wedding party, and Julie's mother and her friend, waited outside the church to throw birdseed at the newlyweds. Julie wanted birdseed instead of the usual rice for the safety of the birds. Matt's car was decorated by his nephews who had a little sense of humor. Julie's mother insisted on paying for Matt and Julie to have a little honeymoon at a local bed and breakfast. So Matt and Julie said how grateful they were for everything and said their goodbyes and they drove two blocks to the "Warrenton Hotel Bed & Breakfast."

The next day Matt and Julie had planned a very special errand that they needed to do. They put Sam in the car with them and they drove out to their new-old house in the country. When they got out of the car, Sam knew the way, and they followed him to the house. Matt had his backpack on that held some very special items, one of the items in particular was very heavy. They followed the old deer path to the site where little baby Angel was buried. They got busy cleaning the area around the stones that looked like a cross. When they were all finished, Julie got a plastic bag out of the backpack which held the gardenia's that were in her wedding bouquet. She carefully placed the gardenias on top of the precious cross which Joe's made of stones. Then Matt put a specially made heavy plaque near the top of the stones and next to the tree. The plaque, which had golden letters on the front read, "Here lies a special little Angel who was born and sadly died on July 14, 1853. She is now with God up in Heaven."

"I think we did a great job what do you think Julie?"

"We sure did Preacher." Julie responded with tears in her eyes as Matt held her close in his arms.

The End

In memory of Matthew Garlock 1971- 1971

Contributions & Acknowledgments

The 1849 Bible that I found in an antique store was amazing. Without it I couldn't have written this book.

My current New International Version Bible, which I used for references, and have proudly read from Genesis to Revelation three times.

History of Trade, plantations, colonialism and colonization in the 13 colonies.

History of slavery on plantations.

My new best friend, The Calculator site, to convert Roman numerals.

I would especially like to thank my dear husband for his love, patience and support for my writing of this book.

Last, but first in my life, I want to thank God.

About the Author

Susan M. Garlock lives in the beautiful state of Minnesota with her husband, two English Setters and a crazy Moluccan Cockatoo Parrot.

Other books by this author:

Dog Hollow Lane

Grandma's Van Gogh

Jenny's Rights

Desperate Cries

First Place Faith

Moonpie

God is always with us no matter what.

Susan M. Garlock

Made in the USA
Charleston, SC
16 January 2015